Joe Flacco

By David Aretha

Consultant: Barry Wilner
AP Football Writer

BEARPORT
PUBLISHING

New York, New York

Credits

Cover and Title Page, © Paul Jasienski/AP Images, Steve Ruark/AP Images for Dairy Queen, and Jim Mahoney/AP Images; 4, © Marcio Sanchez/AP Images; 5, © David Drapkin/AP Images; 7, © Jeff Fusco/Stringer/Getty Images; 8, © Rob Carr/AP Images; 9, © Joe Giblin/AP Images; 10, © Paul Spinelli/AP Images; 11, © Nick Wass/AP Images; 12, © Michael Perez/AP Images; 13, © Jeff Roberson/AP Images; 14, © Gail Burton/AP Images; 15, © Ann Heisenfelt/AP Images; 16, © Lisa Poole/AP Images; 17, © Steve Ruark/AP Images for Dairy Queen; 18, © Michal Vitek/Shutterstock; 19, © Baltimore Humane Society; 20, © Paul Sancya/AP Images; 21, © Damian Strohmeyer/AP Images; 22l, © Staff/MCT/Newscom; 22R, © Nick Wass/AP Images.

Publisher: Kenn Goin
Editor: Jessica Rudolph
Creative Director: Spencer Brinker
Photo Researcher: Chrös McDougall
Design: Dawn Beard Creative

Library of Congress Cataloging-in-Publication Data in process at the time of publication (2015).
Library of Congress Control Number: 2014036565
ISBN-13: 978-1-62724-545-6

For more information, write to Bearport Publishing Company, Inc., 45 West 21st Street, Suite 3B, New York, New York 10010. Printed in the United States of America.

10 9 8 7 6 5 4 3 2 1

CONTENTS

Super Joe

It was the third quarter of the 2013 Super Bowl. The Baltimore Ravens had a 28–6 lead over the San Francisco 49ers. Ravens quarterback Joe Flacco knew he was close to victory. Then, suddenly, the stadium went dark. The electricity was out, and the fans and players had no choice but to wait.

Thirty minutes later, the power came back on. The 49ers began an amazing **comeback**, quickly scoring 17 points. Joe, however, didn't panic. Instead, he calmly moved his team up the field with short, accurate passes and handoffs. Twice he guided the Ravens close enough to the **end zone** to score **field goals**. Those field goals made the difference. Baltimore won the game 34–31!

Joe celebrates after leading the Ravens to victory in Super Bowl XLVII (47).

During the Super Bowl, Joe **completed** 22 of his 33 passes for 287 yards (262 m), three touchdowns, and no **interceptions.** After the game, he was named the Super Bowl **MVP**.

The Athletic Flaccos

Joe was born into an athletic family on January 16, 1985, in New Jersey. His grandfathers, parents, and brothers were all terrific at sports. Joe, however, proved to be the best athlete of them all. As a child, he could launch a football like a rocket.

In Joe's high school, most players on the football team were juniors and seniors. However, Joe was good enough to make the team as a freshman. By his sophomore year, he was already a **starter**. Soon, Joe was one of the best high school quarterbacks in the state. In one game, he threw for 471 yards (431 m). That set a record for South Jersey.

When Joe was in high school, a local newspaper named him the area's Scholar Athlete of the Year. That meant he performed well both in sports and in the classroom.

Joe (back row, center) poses with his family in 2008.

Fightin' Blue Hen

After high school, Joe accepted a **scholarship** to play football at the University of Pittsburgh. In two years, though, he had played in only three games. Joe wanted a chance to play more, so he **transferred** to the University of Delaware.

Delaware's football team, the Fightin' Blue Hens, was in a smaller league than Pittsburgh. However, Joe finally had an opportunity to play more and show off his passing skills. Even as opponents tried to tackle him, Joe could calmly zero in on a teammate and throw the ball directly to him. In one game during his senior year, he threw for 434 yards (397 m). After that season, the Baltimore Ravens picked Joe in the first round of the NFL **draft**!

At the 2008 draft, Joe was the 18th pick. Only one quarterback was picked before him.

Joe prepares to hand the ball off
during a 2006 game for Delaware.

Rookie Surprise

In college, Joe hadn't played against the top football players. So the Ravens' coaches wanted to give him time to get used to the bigger, taller players in the NFL. The coaches' plan was to keep Joe on the sidelines and have him learn the ropes in practices. That didn't happen, though. The Ravens' starting quarterback hurt his shoulder just before the 2008–2009 season began. Then the team's **backup** quarterback got sick. That meant Joe was going to be the starter in the very first game of his **rookie** season!

Joe was under a lot of pressure, but he handled it like a pro. In his first game, he helped the Ravens beat the Cincinnati Bengals 17–10. As the season went on, Joe's pinpoint passes led the Ravens to the **playoffs**.

Fans voted Joe as the NFL Rookie of the Year for the 2008–2009 season.

Joe became the first NFL rookie quarterback ever to lead a team to two playoff victories.

A Winning Game

Over the years, Joe has continued to lead the Ravens to victories. He has also gained the respect of his teammates. Ravens coach John Harbaugh says Joe's toughness and leadership set him apart from other quarterbacks. Joe never complains about getting tackled. He always supports his teammates and never tries to take attention away from them. Ravens players know they can trust Joe to make smart decisions on the field. In fact, Joe became the first quarterback to lead his team to the playoffs in each of his first five seasons.

Joe (left) hands the ball off to a teammate during a 2011 game.

Joe high-fives a teammate after the Ravens scored a touchdown against the Kansas City Chiefs in a 2011 playoff game.

One reason Joe is such a successful quarterback is that he is patient. He waits until a teammate is open before passing the ball. Because of this, he never threw more than 12 interceptions in any of his first five seasons.

Polar Bear Plunge

Joe usually avoids attention off the football field. However, he is happy to use his fame to help the people of Maryland. That was the case on a January day in 2011. Joe wanted to bring attention to **Special Olympics** Maryland (SOMD). The Special Olympics provides opportunities for kids and adults with intellectual disabilities to play sports. Joe joined 12,000 people on the shore of the Chesapeake Bay for SOMD's Polar Bear Plunge.

That day, the beach was covered in snow. "You know how cold it is," Joe said. "You realize how crazy it is." Yet Joe and the others jumped into the frigid bay. It may have been crazy, but the event raised $2.1 million for SOMD!

A swimmer at an SOMD Polar Bear Plunge event

Joe coming out of the water at the Polar Bear Plunge

The water in the Chesapeake Bay was 33°F (0.6°C) on the day of the Polar Bear Plunge. That's just above freezing!

Special Efforts

Joe helps SOMD in other ways, too. Sometimes, he raises money for the organization. Other times, he goes to sporting events and visits with the athletes. The organization's biggest event is called the Summer Games. Athletes compete in sports such as tennis and track. Joe tries to attend the Summer Games every year to support and hang out with the athletes. "It's cool to see athletes out there having fun," Joe has said.

A runner crosses the finish line in a Special Olympics race.

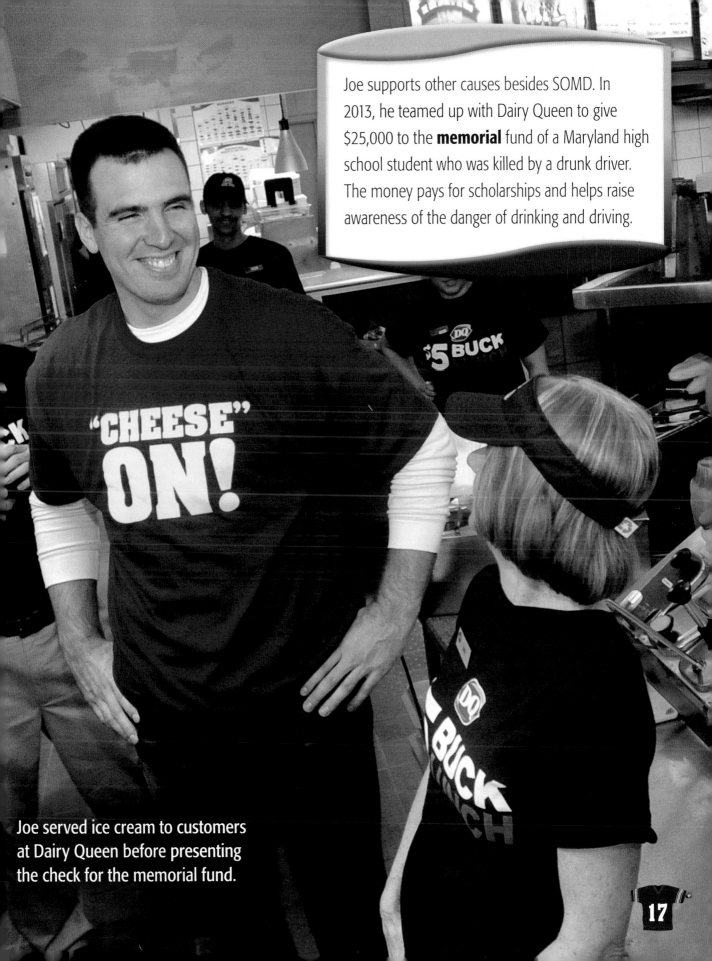

Joe supports other causes besides SOMD. In 2013, he teamed up with Dairy Queen to give $25,000 to the **memorial** fund of a Maryland high school student who was killed by a drunk driver. The money pays for scholarships and helps raise awareness of the danger of drinking and driving.

Joe served ice cream to customers at Dairy Queen before presenting the check for the memorial fund.

A Pet's Best Friend

Another cause close to Joe's heart is helping animals—especially dogs. "I grew up with a deaf white boxer who became a member of our family," he recalls. After joining the Ravens, Joe began working with the Baltimore Humane Society (BHS). The BHS is a no-kill shelter. It doesn't put stray dogs and cats to sleep. Instead, it tries to find homes for them.

In 2012, billboard ads with Joe's picture went up in the Baltimore area. In the photos, he held a puppy and smiled brightly. The ads encouraged people to **adopt** animals, **volunteer** at the BHS, and give money to the shelter.

Joe grew up with a white boxer like this one.

In 2012, Joe hosted an event that raised $9,000 for the BHS. He has also given autographed items to the shelter. People who wanted to win the items had to visit the BHS or "like" the shelter on Facebook.

TEAM UP WITH JOE AND
Baltimore Humane Society

bmorehumane.org

ADOPT · VOLUNTEER · DONATE

A no-kill shelter in Reisterstown, MD

Joe appeared on this billboard ad to support the BHS.

A Leader All Around

Joe has done amazing things for Baltimore. As a quarterback, he helped change how people look at the Ravens. For years, the team was known mostly for having a great defense. Now, with Joe leading the way, the Ravens' offense shines, too. Joe's amazing skills even led the team to a Super Bowl win in 2013.

Joe does more for the city than win football games, though. He also loves to help the people—and animals—of Baltimore. Joe's fans know they can count on him for years to come.

In 2013, Joe passed for a career-high 3,912 yards (3,577 m).

Joe celebrates after throwing a touchdown pass in a 2013 game against the Minnesota Vikings.

The Joe File

Joe is a football hero on and off the field. Here are some highlights.

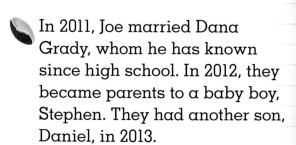

- At the University of Delaware, Joe completed 595 passes during the 26 games he played. That was a school record.

- Joe agreed to appear in the film *Unitas We Stand*, about legendary Baltimore Colts quarterback Johnny Unitas. Joe plays Johnny during the football action scenes.

- In 2011, Joe married Dana Grady, whom he has known since high school. In 2012, they became parents to a baby boy, Stephen. They had another son, Daniel, in 2013.

- Joe's nickname is "Joe Cool" because he stays so calm during games.

Glossary

adopt (uh-DOPT) to take into one's family

backup (BAK-uhp) a player who doesn't play at the start of a game

comeback (KUHM-bak) a situation in which a team that is losing quickly scores many points to close the gap

completed (kuhm-PLEE-ted) caught by one of the team's receivers

draft (DRAFT) an event in which NFL teams choose college players to play for them

end zone (END ZOHN) the area at either end of a football field where touchdowns are scored

field goals (FEELD GOHLZ) scores of three points made by kicking the ball through the goal posts

interceptions (in-tur-SEP-shuhnz) passes caught by players on the defensive team

memorial (muh-MOR-ee-uhl) something that is meant to help remember a person or event

MVP (EM VEE PEE) letters standing for *most valuable player*, an award given to the best player in a game or season

playoffs (PLAY-awfss) final games played to decide which teams will play in a championship

rookie (RUK-ee) a first-year player

scholarship (SKOL-ur-ship) money given to a person so that he or she can go to college

Special Olympics (SPESH-uhl oh-LIM-piks) a group that organizes athletic events for children and adults who have intellectual disabilities

starter (START-ur) a person who plays at the start of a game; the best player at a position

transferred (TRANSS-furd) moved from one school to another

volunteer (vol-uhn-TEER) to do something for no pay to help others

Bibliography

Gormley, Chuck. "Ordinary Joe." *South Jersey Magazine* (March 2009).

Hensley, Jamison. "Rookie QB Flacco Officially Gets Nod for Ravens' Opener." *The Baltimore Sun* (September 2, 2008).

Rosen, Jill. "Ravens Joe Flacco Campaigns for Baltimore Humane Society." *The Baltimore Sun* (January 10, 2012).

Read More

Frisch, Aaron. *Baltimore Ravens (Super Bowl Champions).* Mankato, MN: Creative Education (2011).

Gitlin, Marty. *Joe Flacco: Super Bowl MVP (Playmakers).* Minneapolis, MN: ABDO (2014).

Sandler, Michael. *Joe Flacco and the Baltimore Ravens: Super Bowl XLVII (Super Bowl Superstars).* New York: Bearport (2014).

Learn More Online

To learn more about Joe Flacco and the Baltimore Ravens, visit **www.bearportpublishing.com/FootballHeroes**

Index